Disney
PIRATES of the CARIBBEAN

THE MISSING PIRATE

Printed in the United States of America

First Edition
1 3 5 7 9 10 8 6 4 2

Library of Congress Catalog Card Number: 2006909027

ISBN-13: 978-14231-0621-0
ISBN-10: 1-4231-0621-0

DISNEYPIRATES.COM

THE MISSING
PIRATE

By Jacqueline Ching

Based on characters created for the theatrical motion picture

"Pirates of the Caribbean: The Curse of the Black Pearl"

Screen Story by Ted Elliott & Terry Rossio and Stuart Beattie and Jay Wolpert

Screenplay by Ted Elliott & Terry Rossio

DISNEP
PRESS

New York

Elizabeth Swann grew up in
Port Royal.

Elizabeth's father, Governor Swann,
faced a big problem: pirates!

Pirates attacked ships
heading to Port Royal.

The pirates cut off trade between England and the Caribbean.

"If this doesn't stop, I'll be sent
back to England in disgrace,"
the governor told Elizabeth.

"I must help my father,"
Elizabeth said.
"All you have to do, Miss, is grow
a beard, get a boat, and learn to
sail it," joked Elizabeth's maid.
Elizabeth frowned.

Governor Swann ordered Captain Norrington and the rest of the fleet into action. Norrington was captain of the *Interceptor*.

"Don't worry, Miss Swann.
The *Interceptor* will soon make these
waters safe again," said the captain.

Captain Norrington heard many tales.
But one boat was spoken of more than
any of the others. It was called
the *Cutlass*.
Even pirate ships ran from her.

It wasn't long before the *Interceptor* met up with the *Cutlass*. She must be a pirate ship! Captain Norrington was not going to let her escape.

"But, Captain," a sailor said to Norrington, "the *Cutlass* drives pirates away."

Norrington did not care.
He did not want any ship
taking the law into its own hands.
"Raise the sails and fire when
in range," Norrington commanded.

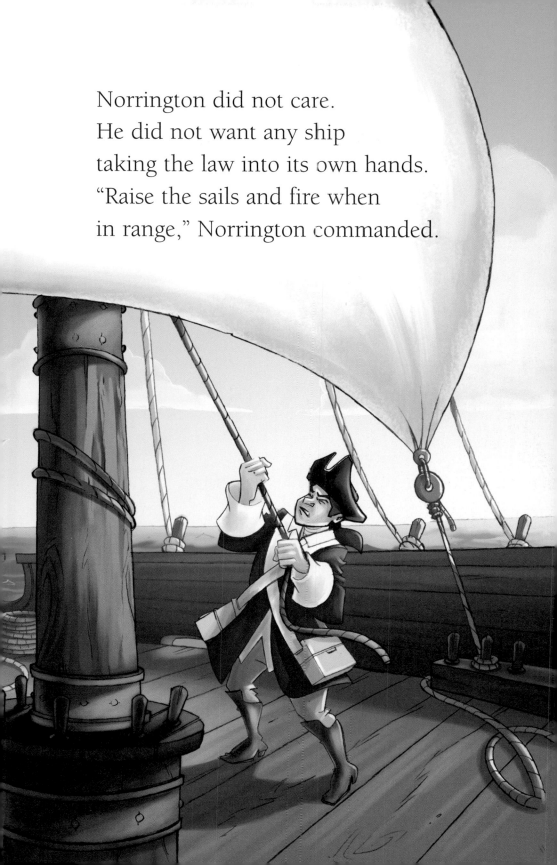

The *Interceptor* found the
Cutlass near the shore.

A hook flew from the *Interceptor* to bring the *Cutlass* closer.

The soldiers on the *Interceptor* drew their swords.

Through his spyglass, Norrington
saw the *Cutlass*. It looked empty.
Then he saw someone in a hat jump
from the ship. It was the captain of the
Cutlass!

"I have never seen a captain
leave his ship!" Norrington said.
The soldiers searched the *Cutlass*.
It was empty. Then they searched
for the captain. He was gone.

Captain Norrington brought
the *Cutlass* back to Port Royal.
The next day he told the governor
about the missing captain.
Governor Swann asked Norrington
to search the *Cutlass*.

When Norrington went down to the
harbor where he had left the boat,
it was gone.
Now, more than ever, he wanted to
catch the pirate captain.

That night, Port Royal awoke to the
sound of cannon blasts!
Captain Norrington raced to his
window. The *Cutlass* was in
the harbor!

"Pirates!" cried Norrington.

The *Cutlass* blasted holes in two pirate ships. The damaged ships fled the harbor.

But the *Cutlass* remained.
Captain Norrington ordered his men
to tow the ship into port.
The soldiers brought the boat in.
"Was the captain aboard?"
Norrington asked.
"No, sir! The ship was empty,"
replied a soldier.

Norrington was angry, but
Governor Swann was happy. He
thought it was Norrington who had
chased away the pirates.

The governor gave Norrington
a reward for a job well done.
The men shook hands.

Meanwhile, the real hero slipped
into Elizabeth's bedroom. It was the
captain of the *Cutlass*!

"You should be proud,"
said Elizabeth's maid,
"you saved your father from disgrace."
"And I didn't have to grow a beard
after all," Elizabeth said.
Elizabeth was the captain of
the *Cutlass*.
She had saved Port Royal!